P9-BZG-120

JANE YOLEN

Grandad Bill's Song

ILLUSTRATED BY

MELISSA BAY MATHIS

PHILOMEL BOOKS ♦ NEW YORK

 Philomel Books, a division of the
Putnam & Grosset Group, 200 Madison Avenue, New York, NY 10016.
Philomel Books, Reg. U.S. Pat. & Tm. Off.
Published simultaneously in Canada.
Printed in Hong Kong by South China Printing Co. (1988), Ltd.
Book design by Gunta Alexander. The text is set in Goudy Old Style.

Library of Congress Cataloging-in-Publication Data
Yolen, Jane. Grandad Bill's song / by Jane Yolen; illustrated by Melissa Bay Mathis. p. cm.
Summary: A boy asks others how they felt when his grandfather died and then shares his own feelings.
[1. Death—Fiction. 2. Grief—Fiction. 3. Grandfathers—Fiction. 4. Stories in rhyme.]
I. Mathis, Melissa Bay, ill. II. Title. PZ8.3.Y76Gr 1994 [E]—dc20 92-26199 CIP AC

ISBN 0-399-21802-5
1 3 5 7 9 10 8 6 4 2

First Impression

To Aunt Isabelle and Uncle Harry,
and all our memories of my father, Will—Billy—Bill.
—J. Y.

To the memory of my grandfather,
Emmet Blackburn Bay—a great scientist, doctor and sailor
and a strong ally for a very young artist.
—M. B. M.

Grandma, what did you do on the day Grandad died?
I sat in my porch rocker, child, and I cried.
I looked at the ocean all covered with foam
And thought of my handsome young sailor gone home.

Bill and Isabelle, 1944

Grandad Bill—young?
Young!

As old as your grandaddy Bill got to be,
He was always that handsome young sailor to me.

Uncle Steve, what did you do on the day Grandad died?
I opened the front door and wandered outside.
I stood for a moment beneath the elm tree,
Remembering just how strong Grandad could be.

Bill with Stevie, 1950

Grandad Bill—strong?
Very strong!

Bill working on cabin roof, 1955

When I was a boy, not much older than you,
There was nothing that my daddy Bill could not do.

Mama, what did you do on the day Grandad died?
I looked in the mirror, and then, son, I lied.
I said to myself that my daddy's not dead.
But the mirror looked back at me, shaking its head.

Bill, Stevie and Jane at the beach, 1953

Did the mirror talk?
Oh, yes, it talked.

Jane at kite contest, 1959

It said: "If you love someone deep in your heart,
Then you and that somebody never can part."

Mr. Temple, what did you do on the day Grandad died?
I went to the window and opened it wide.
I shouted his name, just as if he could hear,
And suddenly felt that your grandad was near.

Bill and Sam Temple, 1946

Near?
Right here.

Bill and Sam at the cabin, 1985

Here by my hand when I move every pawn,
Here in my heart, where he'll never be gone.

My childhood remains in my heart and my head,
And nothing can change that, though Billy is dead.

Daddy, what did you do on the day Grandad died?
Well, I was the one on whom family relied,
So I didn't have time, right at first, to feel sad.
There was so much to do to help out your grandad.

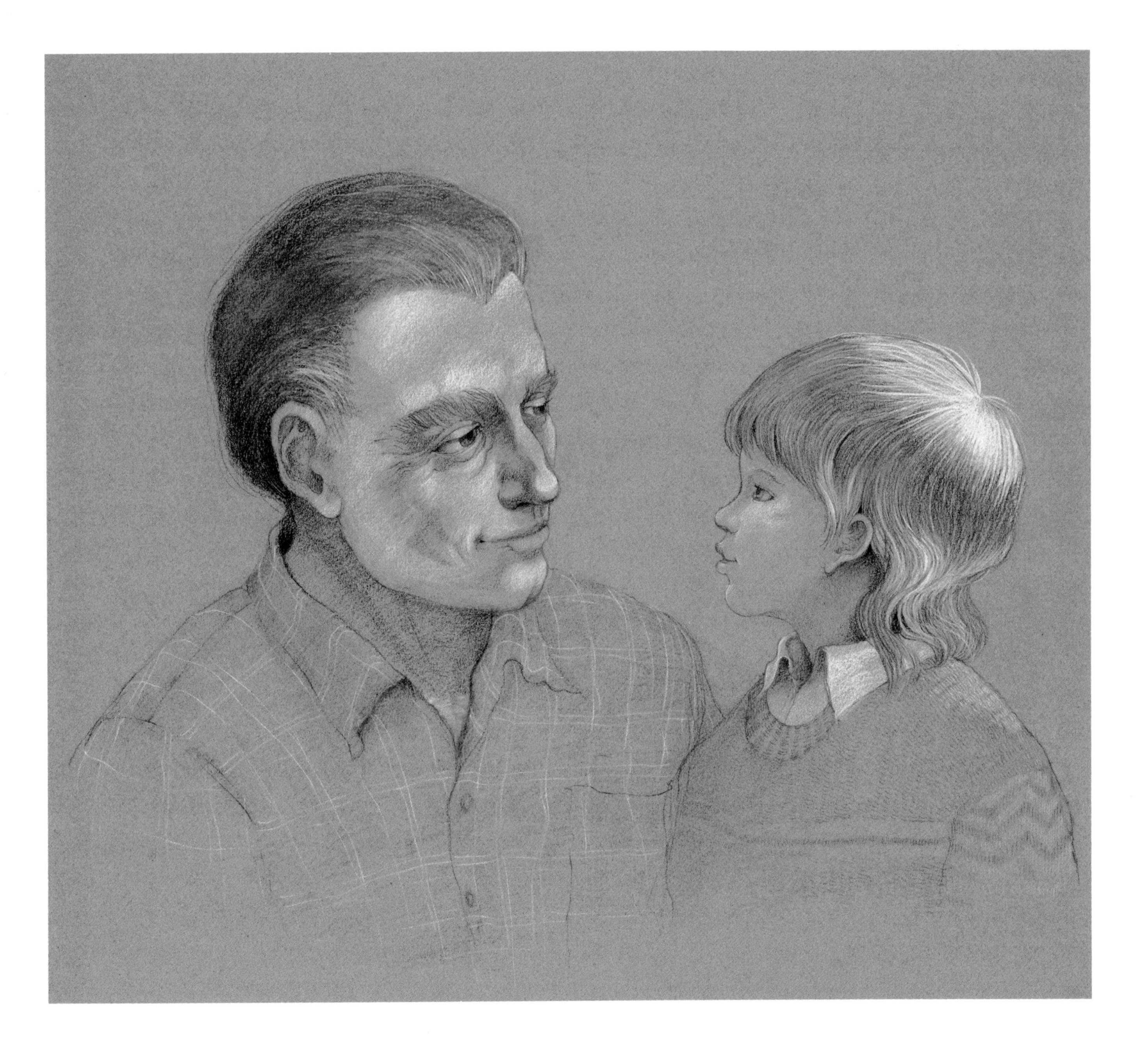

Help? But he was dead.
He still needed things, son.
He needed his best suit, he needed a grave.
I only had time to act strong and be brave.

But that's not how I felt.
Nobody knows how *I* felt.

How did you feel?
I can't tell you. It wasn't nice. It wasn't good.
I wish you would.

Son, what did you do on the day Grandad died?
I wanted to kick out. I wanted to hide.
I hated somebody, I couldn't think who.
There was nothing I wanted to see or to do.

Nothing at all?
Nothing!
So you were mad.
I should have been sad.

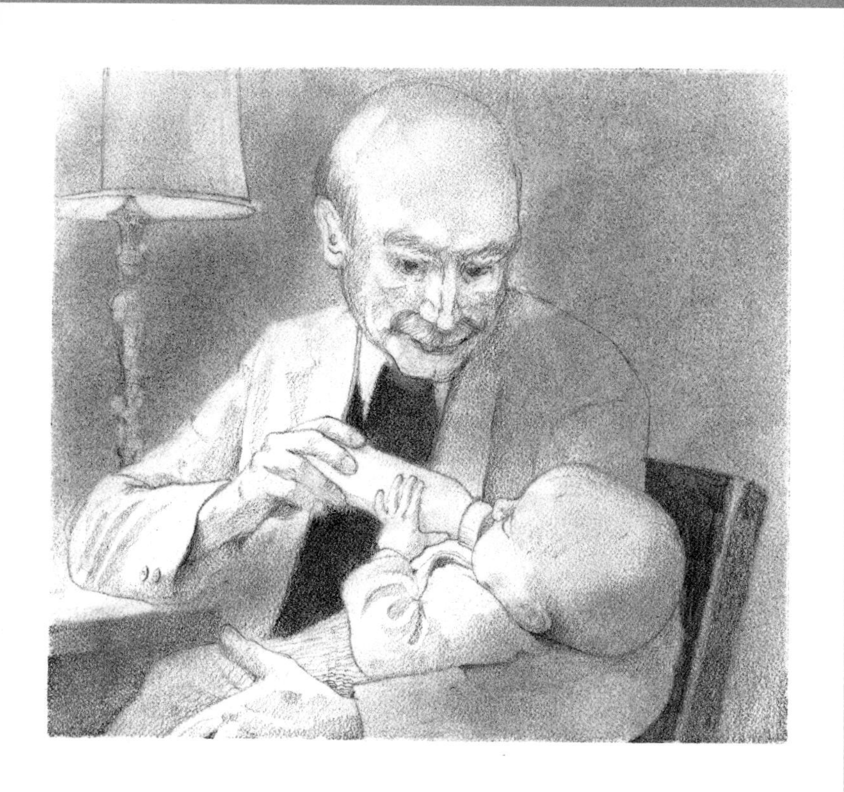

Bill meets Jon for the first time, 1986

Jon with Jessie - his birthday present from Grandad Bill!

Jon, Bill and Jessie
fishing at the cabin, 1991

I think…I think I wanted to…
Yes?
To tell someone something.

You wanted to talk to your own grandad Bill.
And deep in your heart, you are doing that—still.